Dear Parent:
Your child's love of reading starts here!

Every child learns to read in a different way and at his or her own speed. Some go back and forth between reading levels and read favorite books again and again. Others read through each level in order. You can help your young reader improve and become more confident by encouraging his or her own interests and abilities. From books your child reads with you to the first books he or she reads alone, there are I Can Read Books for every stage of reading:

SHARED READING
Basic language, word repetition, and whimsical illustrations, ideal for sharing with your emergent reader

BEGINNING READING
Short sentences, familiar words, and simple concepts for children eager to read on their own

READING WITH HELP
Engaging stories, longer sentences, and language play for developing readers

READING ALONE
Complex plots, challenging vocabulary, and high-interest topics for the independent reader

ADVANCED READING
Short paragraphs, chapters, and exciting themes for the perfect bridge to chapter books

I Can Read Books have introduced children to the joy of reading since 1957. Featuring award-winning authors and illustrators and a fabulous cast of beloved characters, I Can Read Books set the standard for beginning readers.

A lifetime of discovery begins with the magical words "I Can Read!"

Visit www.icanread.com for information on enriching your child's reading experience.

I Can Read Book® is a trademark of HarperCollins Publishers.

Justice League: I Am the Flash
Copyright © 2014 DC Comics.
JUSTICE LEAGUE and all related characters and elements are trademarks of and © DC Comics.
(s14)

HARP30052
Printed in the United States of America. No part of this book may be used or reproduced in any manner whatsoever without written permission except in the case of brief quotations embodied in critical articles and reviews. For information address HarperCollins Children's Books, a division of HarperCollins Publishers, 10 East 53rd Street, New York, NY 10022.
www.icanread.com

Library of Congress catalog card number: 2013940684
ISBN 978-0-06-221005-0

I Can Read!

READING 2 WITH HELP

I Am
the
Flash

by John Sazaklis
pictures by Steven E. Gordon
colors by Eric A. Gordon

HARPER

An Imprint of HarperCollinsPublishers

Meet Barry Allen.

He lives in Central City.

He works as a scientist

at the Central City

Police Department.

Barry also has a big secret.

A few years ago,
Barry was working late
inside the police lab.
Outside, there was a
raging thunderstorm.

Suddenly, a bolt of lightning crashed through the window!

Many different chemicals
spilled onto Barry's body.
The special combination
had a strange effect on him.

Barry's legs began to tingle.
Before he knew it,
the young scientist
was running out the door!

Barry ran all the way home

in less than a minute.

The accident had given him

the power of super-speed.

Barry decided to protect

Central City with his new ability.

He created a special suit

to hide his true identity.

Barry became the Flash—

the Fastest Man Alive!

As time went on,

Barry fine-tuned his powers.

He could run up walls!

He could run on water!

Barry could spin his arms so fast that they created whirlwinds.

The crooks and criminals of
Central City were no match
for this speedy new super hero.

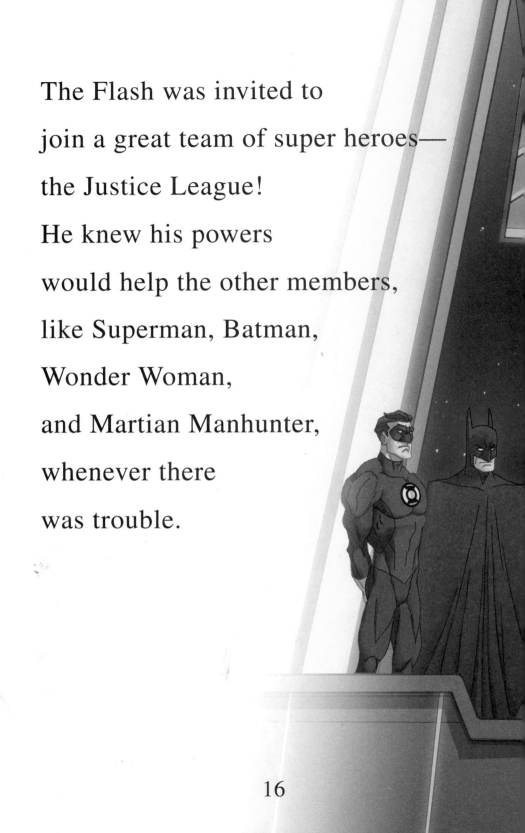

The Flash was invited to
join a great team of super heroes—
the Justice League!
He knew his powers
would help the other members,
like Superman, Batman,
Wonder Woman,
and Martian Manhunter,
whenever there
was trouble.

Barry is working
when he sees a breaking
news report on the television.
All of the super-villains
have broken out of jail!

"It's time to speed things up,"

Barry says.

In the blink of an eye,

Barry becomes the Flash!

The Flash calls the Justice League.
Then he zooms to the prison.
Ultra-Humanite is behind the escape.
The mad scientist implanted his brain
into the body of a mutant ape,
making himself a fierce enemy.

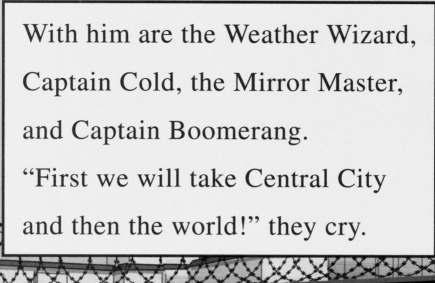

With him are the Weather Wizard, Captain Cold, the Mirror Master, and Captain Boomerang.

"First we will take Central City and then the world!" they cry.

"All you're taking is a trip
back to jail," says the Flash.
"You cannot fight us alone!"
shouts Ultra-Humanite.

"That is why I got a little help
from my friends," replies the Flash.
The Justice League arrives—
ready for action!

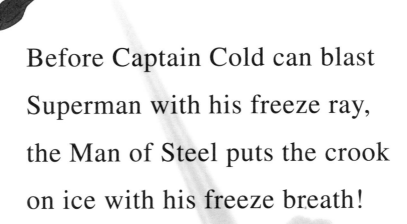

Before Captain Cold can blast
Superman with his freeze ray,
the Man of Steel puts the crook
on ice with his freeze breath!

The Weather Wizard attacks
Batman with his weather wand.
Quickly, the Caped Crusader
knocks him out with a Batarang.

Captain Boomerang is
no match for Wonder Woman.
She ties him up with her
Golden Lasso of Truth.

The Mirror Master uses tricks to try
to fool Martian Manhunter.
The hero uses his mental powers
to take down the crafty crook.

Finally, the Flash goes up
against Ultra-Humanite.
"I will pound you into the ground!"
growls the mutant gorilla.

"Catch me if you can!" says the Flash.

"Keep your eyes on the moving target!"

He zigs and he zags and he zooms

swiftly around Ultra-Humanite.

The Scarlet Speedster zips faster and faster and faster in a big circle. The extreme speed creates a tornado that lifts the villains up into the air. The strong winds send the criminals spiraling over the prison wall, back to where they came from. "Thanks for your help, my friends," the Flash says to the Justice League. "Central City is safe once again."

"Bad guys had better beware,"
says the hero.
"I am the protector of Central City.
I am the Fastest Man Alive.
I am the Flash!"